THE SESAME STREET ABC STORYBOOK

FEATURING JIM HENSON'S MUPPETS

WRITTEN BY

Jeffrey Moss

Norman Stiles

Daniel Wilcox

ILLUSTRATED BY

Peter Cross   Michael Frith

Tim and Greg Hildebrandt

Joe Mathieu   Marc Nadel

RANDOM HOUSE • CHILDREN'S TELEVISION WORKSHOP

CONTENTS

a A

An A Story

Once upon a time, in a far-away kingdom, there lived a queen named Queen Agatha. One day, Queen Agatha called all the knights of the kingdom to the throne room.

I love things that begin with A!

4

"Knights of the kingdom," announced Queen Agatha, "I love things that begin with A. Whoever can bring me something that begins with the letter A will be rewarded handsomely. *Perhaps* the winner will dance with me at the royal party tonight."

"Oh, boy!" said Sir Bird. "I'm heading for the Royal Zoo! That's the only place where I can find something that begins with the letter A. I'll be right back, Queen Agatha!"

Sir Bird hurried from the throne room, pausing only long enough to take an apple from a bowl near the throne room door.

"I'd better bring this apple with me," he said, "in case I get hungry on my way to the zoo."

Once outside the castle, Sir Bird realized that he was lost.

"Oh, no, I'm lost!" cried Sir Bird. "If only there were something to help me find my way to the Royal Zoo."

Just then, Sir Bird passed a large arrow. The arrow said, "This way to the zoo."

"Oh, look at that arrow!" exclaimed Sir Bird. "That arrow will help me find my way."

This way to the ZOO

So he grabbed the arrow and followed it until he reached his destination—a cage in the Royal Zoo where there sat a happy-looking alligator.

"Oh, Mr. Alligator, I've found you at last," said Sir Bird. "Your name begins with the letter A. Won't you please come with me, back to the throne room?"

Since the alligator had never before seen a throne room, he was more than happy to follow Sir Bird.

When he reached the throne room,
Sir Bird announced to the Queen,
"Queen Agatha, this alligator's name
begins with the letter A. I guess
now I can dance with you
at the royal party,
huh?"

"Well," said the Queen,
"first of all that apple and that arrow
you have also begin with the letter A."

"Oh, how silly of me!" said Sir Bird. "I grabbed the apple
and the arrow without realizing that they began with
the letter A. But I guess that since I brought you an apple
and an arrow and an alligator, I can dance with you at the
royal party for sure."

The building belonged to a giant named Burly Barney. Burly Barney was in the bedroom eating his breakfast of bushels of buttered buns, barrels of blueberries and bunches of bananas. When Bert saw how big Burley Barney was, Bert beat it to the back room.

There, Bert found a big basket. It was full of bottlecaps.

"Boy, oh boy, oh boy!" said Bert. "Bottlecaps! I collect bottlecaps!"
So Bert brought the basket of bottlecaps back to the beanstalk.

But Burley Barney saw Bert, and he began to bellow, "You took my bottlecaps!" "I'd better beat it," said Bert.

10

Boldly, Bert climbed down. Barney bounded down behind him. But, on a bottom branch, Bert slipped and fell with a bump.

"I'll bet you want to bash me because I borrowed your basket of bottlecaps," blurted Bert.

"Are you batty?" bellowed Burley Barney. "Those bottlecaps are boring! They were driving me bananas! Thank you for borrowing my bottlecaps!"

And Burley Barney shook Bert's hand. In fact, he shook Bert's whole body. Then Barney bounded back up the beanstalk to his beautiful black building.

And now that the basket of bottlecaps belonged to Bert, Bert had the best and biggest bunch of bottlecaps on the block. So Bert was beaming.

And everyone lived blissfully ever after. Except Ernie . . . who was bored.

Oh, brother— that's BORING!

c C A Poem by Cookie Monster

C is for COOKIES.
Me like them a bunch.
Me crunch them for dinner
And breakfast and lunch.

And then there are CRUMBS.
Cookie crumbs are so yummy!
Me sweep them off table
And into my tummy.

Did you know
   the word CARTON
   begins with a C?
That's the box
   cookies come in.
It tastes good to me! !

Well, that's all the C words
Me got for today.
Me get in my car now
And me drive away.

Hey, wait!

The word CAR starts with C.
Boy, that's neat!
Me thought me had run out of
C things to eat.

CRUNCH!

CRUNCH!

CRUNCH!

Tasty—
But not as good as
COOKIE!

Bye-bye!

If you listen closely to the next story, you'll see that it's filled with words that begin with the letter F. It's called . . .

F f

...The Fable of Fat Fireman Foster

Once upon a time, there was a famous fireman named Fat Fireman Foster. Fat Fireman Foster was famous because he was a fabulous fire fighter and because all his names began with the letter F.

One Friday in February, Fat Fireman Foster was driving his fancy fire truck through a forest when all of a sudden he saw some smoke! "Where there's smoke, there's fire!" said Fat Fireman Foster. "And since this is a forest, that must be a forest fire! Never fear," called Fat Fireman Foster. "Fat Fireman Foster is here!"

In a flash, Fat Fireman Foster fetched his fire hose. He pointed it at the smoke and turned it on. FLOOSH! "I have flooded the forest fire and it is finished," said Fat Fireman Foster.

But when the smoke cleared, Fat Fireman Foster found that it had not been a forest fire at all!

17

"Oh, no!" said Fat Fireman Foster. "I figured it was a forest fire—but it was a frankfurter fire instead! Just a few friendly folks fixing frankfurters! Oh, I'm sorry, folks," said Fat Fireman Foster. "Can you ever forgive me?"

"Sure, we'll forgive you!" said the folks. "We still have our frankfurters. And we have our fins and flippers, too. Fortunately we know how to swim and eat at the same time. Come join the fun, Fat Fireman Foster!"

So Fat Fireman Foster joined the fun and had a fabulous time feeding on frankfurters and flipping the flippers he borrowed from his new-found friends.

There are two things to be learned from the fable of Fat Fireman Foster:

Number one is:
Sometimes things are not
what you think they are.

Number two is:
The names Fat, Fireman,
and Foster all begin
with the letter F.

18

22

The Count Inks an I

Greetings!

I am the Count. I am here in this Alphabet Book to show you the letter **I**. I will make the letter **I** with this ink. **Ink** begins with the letter **I**. But I'll bet you knew that already.

There! This is the letter **I**. One poor lonely letter **I**. I will make another.

There!
Two letter **I**'s.
Ha. Ha. Ha.
Now, let me
see…

Four thousand, two hundred
and twenty-one
letter **I**'s...

Four thousand, two
hundred and twenty-two
letter **I**'s...

Oh, it's WONDERFUL!

Ha, ha, ha.

Four thousand, two hundred
and twenty-three...

j J

The Jolly Juggler

There is a jolly juggler
Who juggles every day.
She can juggle lots of things
That all begin with J.

She can juggle jugs and jacks
And jars of jelly, too.
And if your name begins with J
She'll even juggle you.

'Cause she can juggle Johnnies,
And Janes and Joels and Jills.
Ooops, there's been a big mistake—
Hey, wait…my name is Bill!

The Pied Kazoo-er of Kamlin

Once upon a time, there was a town named Kamlin. And Kamlin had a problem. Kamlin had too many kangaroos.

Kamlin had kangaroos everywhere. Kangaroos in the kitchens. Kangaroos in the kindergarten. Kangaroos in the keyholes. Uptown, downtown, and midtown, there were kangaroos, kangaroos, kangaroos!

J. Mathie

The townspeople couldn't stand it. So they had a town meeting. Mayor Kinkaid made a speech. She said, "We've got too many kangaroos!" And everybody cheered.

Then she said, "We need a plan!" And everybody stopped cheering. Because nobody had a plan. So they all sat there, thinking very hard.

Then up walked a keen-eyed stranger. He was dressed from head to foot in patchwork, and under his arm he carried a long kazoo.

"My friends," he said, "I am the Pied Kazoo-er, and I have the key to your kangaroo problem."

"Are you kidding?" said a townsperson. "How can you solve our kangaroo problem? By playing your kazoo?"

"Yes," said the Pied Kazoo-er, smiling mysteriously, and he raised his kazoo to his lips. Instantly, the air was filled with strange and enchanting music.

Then something magical happened. As the Pied Kazoo-er walked along, playing his kazoo, people began to follow him. All the people on King Street followed him. All the people on Kite Hill followed him. All the people who heard his bewitching music followed him.

In fact, all the people in the whole town of Kamlin followed him. They followed him out of Kamlin to a kingdom far away, where they never saw another kangaroo again.

When the people left, the kangaroos took over the town of Kamlin. They made it a kangaroo town. It became busy and prosperous, and soon it was the biggest, most famous kangaroo town in the world.

And the kangaroos lived happily ever after. So did the people.

And, by the way, just in case you didn't notice: Kamlin, and kangaroo, and kazoo . . . and lots of other words in this story, too . . . all start with the letter K. It's true. See for yourself.

L¹

The Legend of Lasso Louise

35

Hello.

I, Grover, am going to tell you some poems all about three friends of mine. And their names all begin with the letter **O**.

I like Ogden Ox . . .
he really is neat.

Except when he's dancing and steps on my feet.

37

Olive the Octopus
has many charms.

Except when she hugs me
with all of her arms.

OH
OH!

Ollie the Ostrich
is very well bred.

Except when he's tired
and sits on my head.

Well, those are all the **O** poems
I have time for today. I do not
think I am going to do any more
for a long, long time. Good-by.
O o o o o o o o o o o o o h.

39

The Story of Pete the Pirate

Once upon a time, a nasty pirate sailed into a town. "Ahoy, mateys," the pirate announced. "My name is Pete the Pirate, and I am so nasty that I am going to take away everything in your town that begins with the letter **P**."

And immediately, he grabbed a bag of **peanuts** from the hand of a little girl and dropped it into his pirate sack.

"Heh, heh," chuckled Pete the Pirate, and before he had finished chuckling, he had grabbed a **pizza pie** from the hands of a pizza-maker and had thrown it into his pirate sack.

"There's only one thing you can do to stop me from taking all the **P** things in your town," said Pete the Pirate. "And that's to say a special word that begins with the letter **P**. If anyone says the special **P** word, then I'll stop and go away."

And with that, he picked up a little boy's **puppy** and threw it into his pirate sack.

40

The people of the town got together and tried to think of what the special **P** word might be. The mayor had an idea. So he marched right up to Pete the Pirate and announced, "**Pickle**!"

"**Pickle**?" said Pete the Pirate. "You think that's the word that will make me stop? Ha!"

And he grabbed the mayor's **pants** right off him and threw them into his pirate sack.

Then, just for good measure, he grabbed the **packages** from the arms of a passing lady, and a stray **pig** that was walking down the street. He threw them in his pirate sack, too.

41

The people of the town got together again to try to think of the special **P** word that would make the pirate stop taking things. The cook from the biggest restaurant in town had an idea. So when the pirate came into his kitchen, the cook yelled, "**Porcupine**!"

"**Porcupine**?" said the pirate. "You think that's the special word that will make me stop? You're a pretty silly cook, you know that?"

And with that, the pirate grabbed all the cook's **pots** and **pans** and threw them into his pirate sack. Then, just for good measure, he went through the town collecting all the **pillows** and **pianos** and threw them into his pirate sack, too.

Well, the people of the town were getting pretty upset when a little boy came up to the pirate just as he was pulling a **pair** of **pajamas** off the washline.

"Mr. Pirate," said the little boy, "won't you stop taking all the **P** things from our town?"

"Why should I?" said the pirate. "I'm nasty."

"*Please*," said the little boy.

"What did you say?" said the pirate.

"I said *please*," said the little boy.

"That's it!" exclaimed the pirate. "That's the special word. **Please** is the special **P** word! I don't like you at all, little boy, but I'll have to stop because you said **please**."

And as quickly as Pete the Pirate had come to town, he left — and he never came back again.

The townspeople were grateful to the little boy. They only wished they had thought of the special **P** word sooner. Still, with the pirate gone, things could return to normal, and the people of the town all lived pretty happily ever after.

Rr

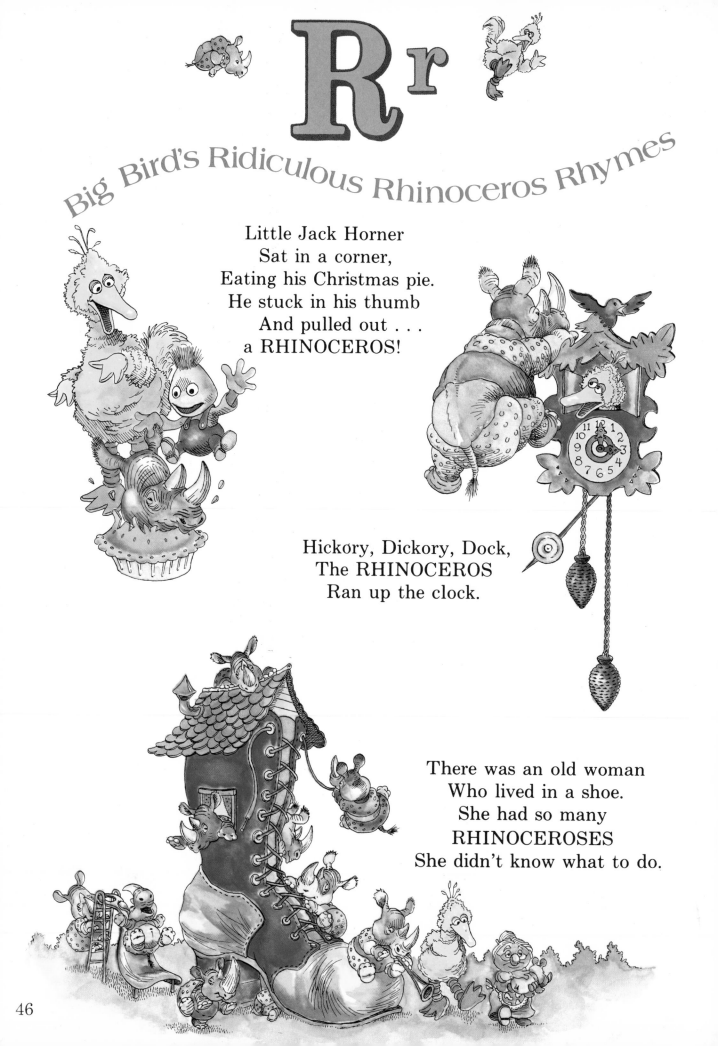

Big Bird's Ridiculous Rhinoceros Rhymes

Little Jack Horner
Sat in a corner,
Eating his Christmas pie.
He stuck in his thumb
And pulled out . . .
a RHINOCEROS!

Hickory, Dickory, Dock,
The RHINOCEROS
Ran up the clock.

There was an old woman
Who lived in a shoe.
She had so many
RHINOCEROSES
She didn't know what to do.

46

Sing a song of sixpence,
A pocket full of
RHINOCEROSES!

Old Mother Hubbard went
to the cupboard
To get her poor dog a bone.
But when she got there, she found . . .
a RHINOCEROS!

Ridiculous Rhinoceros Rhymes
may be silly, but RHINOCEROS
begins with the letter R, and
that's what's really important.

The Sock-maker and the Snuffle-upagus

Ss

*O*nce there was a poor, tired old Sock-maker. One day, he promised to sew socks for the whole town, but by evening he was just too tired to finish.

Oh, dear. I can't sew another sock. I hate to disappoint everybody, but I have to go to sleep. Goodnight, Big Bird.

Gee, poor Mr. Sock-maker.

SOCKS BOX

HILDEBRANDT

Suddenly, there was a strange sound, a puff
of smoke, and a flash of light, and there
before Big Bird stood the Snuffle-upagus fairy.

Who are you?

I am the
Snuffle-upagus
fairy. I watch
over poor, tired
sock-makers
everywhere.

The Snuffle-upagus fairy got right to work.

I'll sew those
socks for him.

Look out! Your
tail knocked
those boxes over!

He sewed all night long.

I don't mean to brag, but I'm sewing some super socks.

Look out! You accidentally bashed in that wall!

And by sunup he had sewn every single sock.

I'm finished! And none too soon.

Look out! You smashed the store window!

And with the same puff of smoke and flash of light, the Snuffle-upagus fairy vanished as quickly as he had appeared.

Gee, do you have to vanish now? Mr. Sock-maker has never seen you, and I'm sure he'd like to meet you.

Sorry, Bird. We Snuffle-upagus fairies never stay to receive thanks.

When the Sock-maker woke up, was he ever surprised!

Why . . . who sewed my socks for me? And, by the way, who destroyed my store?

I can explain. . . . You see, during the night, the Snuffle-upagus fairy came, and he finished the socks, but he accidentally broke everything, and—

51

Oh, not that same
Snuffle-upagus
story again, Big Bird.
There's no such thing
as a Snuffle-upagus.
You have some
imagination!

SOCKS BOX

And even though the Sock-maker didn't believe Big Bird,
they all lived happily ever after . . . as soon as they
had finished cleaning up the store.

T t

The Terrible Tickler

*T*he whole town of Tombstone remembers the day
That the Terrible Tickler came riding their way.
He came down the street with a look keen and steady
And said, "Folks, my tickling finger is ready.
Now tickling's terrific and tickling is fun,
And you'll all be tickled before I am done.
For tickling's my pleasure, my greatest of joys.
I think I'll start off with the young girls and boys!"

He first tickled Teddy,
Then Mike, Fran and Sue,
Then Manuel and Mary
And Algernon, too.
Not one could escape,
Though they'd run and they'd wriggle—
Each one would get tickled
And fall down and giggle.
And soon not a boy
Or a girl could be found
Except those who lay
Laughing down on the ground.

"I've got all the kids. Now it's time for the others,"
The Tickler announced. "Next come fathers and mothers."

So the Terrible Tickler
Went on with his work.
He got Nina the plumber
And Charlie the clerk.
He got Sam the barber
And even the mayor
Who fell laughing and giggling
Right out of his chair.

And as sure as five pennies add up to one nickel,
There wasn't one grownup that he didn't tickle.
"I've tickled the people but still I'm not through."
Said the Terrible Tickler, "Now guess what I'll do."

Well, he tickled the horses
And tickled the cows,
He tickled the cats
Till they giggled meows.
He tickled the pigs
And the mules and the dogs.
And he tickled the chickens
And even the frogs.

Then he looked all around and said, "I'm in a pickle.
I'm done and there's nobody left here to tickle.
I've tickled them all now," he said with a frown.
"I guess I'll just have to go find a new town!"
So he tickled a doll sitting high on a shelf.
Then he rode out of town as he tickled—himself.

And everyone said with a giggle and sigh,
"That Terrible Tickler's a mean rotten guy."
And they heard him call back as he giggled with glee,
"Remember that *tickle begins with a T.*"

Grover Gets Wet

Ww

Hi! It is your old pal Grover again, here to talk to you about the letter **W**.

Do you know what begins with the letter **W**? **Water** begins with the letter **W**. And this is a big tank of water.

Do you know who lives in this tank of water? Willy the Walrus lives in this tank of water. And his name begins with the letter **W**, too. Oh, this is so much fun.

I will now bend over the top of the tank and see if my cute little eyes can see Willy the Walrus.

WHOOPS!

Whoops also starts with the letter W.

Now I am wet. The word **wet** also begins with the letter **W**. Well, since I am wet, there is one other thing that begins with the letter **W** . . .

WASH!

61

Ernie Buys a Z

As Ernie walked down the street one day, he heard a "Pssst!" from nearby. He looked around and saw a shifty-looking Salesman hiding behind a tree.

"C'mere, kid," said the Salesman. "I'm gonna show you something that'll save you pain and trouble." And out from under his coat he took a big letter **Z**.

"That's the letter **Z**," said Ernie. "How will it save me pain and trouble?"

"I'll explain," said the Salesman. "Suppose you're at a party. And suppose somebody at the party asks you what the first letter is in the word **zebra**. And you can't remember."

"Oh, dear," said Ernie. He was imagining the party. He could just see it. Everybody would be pointing at him, and saying he couldn't spell. They'd probably never invite him to another party. If only he could remember the first letter in **zebra**!

"But," said the Salesman, "if you had this **Z**, you could take it out, look at it, and it would remind you that the first letter in **zebra** is **Z**."

"Thank goodness for that **Z**," said Ernie. "It's great for parties."

"Right," said the Salesman. "And there's another way it can help you. Suppose you're on a quiz show. The prize is two million dollars, *plus* a trip around the world, *and* a carton full of rubber duckies . . ."

"Wowee!" said Ernie. "What a prize!"

The Salesman went on, "Your question is: What's the first letter in the word **zoo**? But you can't remember. The seconds are ticking by . . .

. . . the band is playing tense music. . . ."

Ernie could just picture the whole thing. There he was, on the quiz show. If he couldn't answer the question, he'd get no prize! Everybody would boo him! If only he could remember the first letter in **zoo**!

"Well," said the Salesman, "if you had this **Z**, it would remind you that the first letter in zoo is **Z**."

"That settles it!" said Ernie. "I've got to have that **Z**! It'll save me pain and trouble!"

So Ernie bought the **Z** and walked away with it down the street.

The Salesman was about to leave when a stranger came up, holding a microphone. "HI!" he said. "I'm GUY SMILEY, and *you* are on QUIZ SHOW IN THE STREET! Today's prize is TWO MILLION DOLLARS, *PLUS* A TRIP AROUND THE WORLD, *AND* A CARTON FULL OF RAINCOATS! And TODAY'S QUESTION is: WHAT IS THE FIRST LETTER IN THE WORD **ZERO**?"

And to Guy Smiley's surprise, the Salesman ran away down the street shouting, "Hey, kid! Come back here with that letter!"